# ADVENTURES ON CAIRNGORM

CairnGorm Mountain Ltd would like to thank
our local school children for naming
the carriages Coire and Cairn.

Text © Pat Gerber
Illustrations © Sue Gerber

First Published in 2002 by
**Glowworm Books Ltd**. Unit 7, Greendykes Industrial Estate,
Broxburn, West Lothian, EH52 6PG, Scotland
on behalf of CairnGorm Mountain Ltd, Aviemore, Scotland.

Telephone: 01506-857570
Fax: 01506-858100
URL: http://www.glowwormbooks.co.uk

ISBN 1 871512 75 1

Reprint Code    10    9    8    7    6    5    4    3    2    1

Printed and bound in Scotland by Scotprint, Haddington.

# ADVENTURES ON CAIRNGORM

Pat Gerber
Illustrated by Sue Gerber

One breezy day, Coire and Cairn arrive in Aviemore, Scotland.

'What's that noise?' asks Coire.

Cairn says 'Scottish music. Look, it makes people dance and sing.'

'I'd like to dance and sing too,' says Coire.

Cairn snorts, 'That's a daft idea. Trains don't dance and sing. Trains carry people and stuff.'

'Where to?' asks Coire.

Cairn says, 'To – um - stations.'

'What for?' wonders Coire.

Cairn says, 'Because it's too far for them to walk, silly, or they've got things to carry.'

'But how can I carry people anywhere when I don't have an engine?' cries Coire. 'We're not real trains.'

Cairn squeaks, 'Eeeek, I don't have an engine either!'

'Oh no, everyone will laugh at us,' whispers Coire.

Cairn says, 'Don't worry. Something will turn up.'

3

High on the mountain side a cold wind blows. Lots of
people watch as an enormous crane hoists Coire aloft.

'Help!' shrieks Coire. 'Put me down! I'm not an aeroplane.'
Cairn shouts, 'Look at me! I'm
flying like a bird. Wheeeee!'

The crane pops Coire neatly onto the
track. Soon Cairn is on the track too. Everyone
crowds round to watch.
'I don't know any of these people,' says
Coire shyly. 'What if they don't like us?'
Cairn says, 'Don't worry, they're only
staring because we're new here. But we're going
to carry them up that hill in six minutes, all cosy and
dry. They'll love us.'
'That very very high hill? Oh no, but I'm scared of
heights,' wails Coire.

4

Up in the control room, Eric the Engineer and his mates are hard at work. 'We'll soon have Coire and Cairn running like clockwork. These two big electric engines are really strong.'

Stroma the Driver says, 'Strong enough to pull two trains?'

Eric explains, 'Sure. The engines work the cable that pulls Coire and Cairn up and down.'

Stroma asks, 'How do I stop Coire at the stations?'

'We've brakes here in the control room,' says Eric. 'And Coire and Cairn each have three extra brakes, in case they need to stop suddenly. Exactly halfway down, the track divides into two, so the two trains can pass each other safely.'

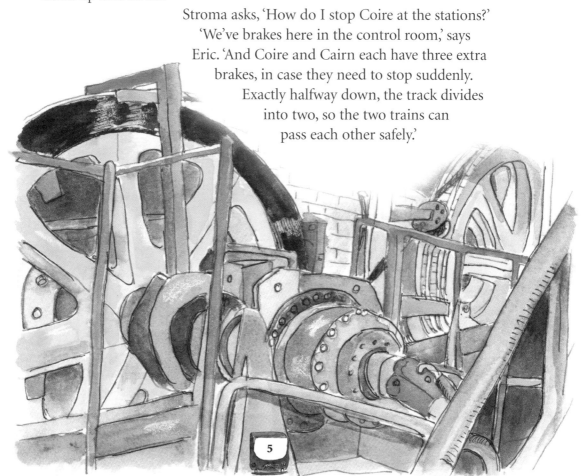

It is the trains' first day of work. Cairn passes Coire, boasting, 'I got to take the Very Important People up for my first journey.'

'V.I.P.s? Boring. I'm full of cheery children,' laughs Coire, trundling onwards up the hill.

Cairn calls, 'Children, eh? You'll have no problem lifting them up the next bit, then. It's quite steep.'

6

'Oh dear,' wails Coire, seeing
what a big hill lies ahead. 'Maybe
I won't make it up there.'
Cairn calls, 'Yes you will. I'm going down for
more passengers. See you next trip. Watch out
for the tunnel. Byeeeee.'

7

The strong cable pulls the little train safely up the steep mountainside.
A black hole lies ahead. 'Anyone would think I was a rabbit,' thinks Coire,
plunging in.

'Oh, it's very very dark
in here.'

Stroma the Driver
keeps a steady hand
on the controls. The
children are silent,
waiting.

Then far, far away, a small circle of light appears at the end of the tunnel.
The light grows bigger and bigger.

Here they are in the Top Station. 'Made it!' hoots Coire.

'The doors are opening,' says an automatic voice.

Stroma the Driver stands by the doors as the children leave the train. They're laughing and chattering as they follow each other up the stairs.

Some will take a look round the Shop at the Top, others will explore the Exhibition. Then maybe they'll all enjoy yummy drinks and food in the Ptarmigan Restaurant.

For several days all goes well. Coire and Cairn pull each other up the hill, turn about all day long, carrying children, grownups and all sorts of things up to the Top Station and bringing some of them down again. Till one day someone drops a spanner in the works. There's a flash and a bang and everything stops.

'Help!' wails Coire.
'Help, I'm stuck.'

Cairn calls, 'Where's Eric the Engineer?'
Stroma the Driver wrestles with the controls. 'He's on his lunch break.'
'Ohhhh, this is so scary,' squeaks Coire, stuck on the steepest bit of the track.
Soon the rescue teams appear. Coire's passengers are hoisted safely out.

Eric the Engineer rushes in to the control room. Whap! He fixes the engine. 'Sorry. Only a technical hitch,' he says, finishing his sandwich.

All winter long the trains work hard, toiling up and down
CairnGorm Mountain carrying skiers, snowboarders
and sightseers. At night, Eric the Engineer and his
team check everything over, to keep Coire and
Cairn in good working order.

11

By the time Spring comes, the animals and
birds have become used to the trains and are too busy
nesting and rearing their young to pay much heed to them.
It is the Easter holidays. A group of children come to explore
CairnGorm with the Countryside Ranger.

Coire says, 'What are they looking for?'

'They've come to look at the rocks, birds and wild flowers
that are so special to this mountain,' says Cairn.

12

Cairn explains, 'No more skiers. The snow's almost gone. The Middle Station's closed. We'll have different passengers now.'

'No more wet melty slush from all these skiers. I'm beginning to like it here,' whispers Coire, basking in the sunshine.

Cairn says, 'Yes, and I like it now we're up to full speed – thirty six kilometres an hour! That's fast for a funicular. In fact we're the fastest funiculars in the universe.'

Greetings from Cairngorm

wood ant

cross-leaved heath

crowberry

twinflower

bell heather

juniper

ptarmigan

14

Summer comes and the mountain grasses turn green. Flowers grow among the boulders and the animals bring out their young for the first time.

Summer visitors from all over the world come to visit CairnGorm Mountain. There are scientists, mountaineers, bird-watchers, ramblers, photographers, film makers, actors and an artist. As well as enjoying the mountain from walks at the base, many are delighted to find Coire and Cairn able to carry them up to the Ptarmigan Centre.

red deer

golden eagle

One late afternoon at the Base Station,
big notices are put up;
'SATURDAY 18TH MAY 2002
FUNICULAR RAILWAY CLOSED
DUE TO FUNCTION'.

'I've seen a big white scary ghost,' puffs
Coire, passing Cairn at the Middle Station.
'What's worse, it's in my third compartment.
Look!'

Cairn snorts, 'That's not a ghost. That's a bride.
There's to be a wedding at the top station.'

'Eeeek, I've just recognised her,' yells Coire. 'It's my
driver, Stroma!'

Cairn giggles, 'Correct. I've just taken
David the bridegroom up. He's
waiting there for her. Better
hurry.

SATURDAY 18TH MAY 2002
FUNICULAR RAILWAY
CLOSED
DUE TO FUNCTION

They're having the
first ever Mountain
Railway wedding in
Scotland.'

   After the wedding reception
party, Coire brings everyone down the
hill. It's very late and the sun has gone
down.

   'Oh I'm so tired,' yawns Coire. 'Time for a shower.'
   The cleaners soon have both trains spick and span
and everyone goes home.

One night in
June, CairnGorm
Mountain falls silent.
There isn't a single car left in
the car park. Only the moon moves
slowly across the night sky.

'Bing-bong,' goes the intercom. Cairn rings down from
the top station. 'Fancy a Midsummer Eve dance?'

'If you're
asking,' laughs Coire.
'I'd like to go off the rails, for
a change.'
Cairn giggles, 'Come fly with me.'
'Let's fly, let's fly away,' sings Coire, taking to the air.
Cairn yells, 'I'm a helicopter, look at me – whirrrrrrrr!'
'I'm a bird,' warbles Coire. 'Oh for the wings, for the
wings of a dove!'
But, by the time the early morning sun peeps over the mountain side,
everything is as it was. Coire and Cairn are ready for the new day's
passengers as if nothing had happened.

Rothiemurchus

September
S M T W Th F S
1 2 3 4 5 6 7
8 9 10 11 12 13 14
15 16 17 18 19 20 21
22 23 24 25 26 27 28
29 30

After a busy summer season, September comes. The visitors from other countries go home. All over Scotland, pupils are busy at school. From Monday to Friday, pensioners, grannies and grandpas, aunties, uncles and retired teachers come walking and rambling around the slopes of CairnGorm. Lots of them clamber aboard Coire and Cairn and go up to the Top Station to see the view and shop and eat. The animals and birds begin to prepare for Autumn. Some will stay, others will fly away to warmer lands.

Every weekend, families and friends come to explore the mountain. There are rock climbers, botanists, geologists and people from the city just wanting a bit of good fresh air.

Soon it's the October holiday. A party of children, with their teachers,
are here to try a mountain scramble. They're halfway up a cliff when a
great storm begins. Soon it's blowing a blizzard and no-one can
see anything, except the little purple trains toiling up and
down the track.

Suddenly a boy is blown off the rock. Crash!
He falls to the ground.

The leader phones for
help. He ropes all the
other children together
so no-one gets lost.

Cairn is stuck. 'What's
up Coire? Not another
spanner in the works?'

'That wee boy needs help,' hoots
Coire. 'He's badly hurt. I'm not
budging till they bring him aboard. You'll
just have to hang on and be patient.'

Cairn grumbles, 'I've a load of folk up
there waiting to be collected. They've a bus to catch.'

At last the Mountain Rescue Team arrive. They tie the injured climber
onto a stretcher and carry him to the train. Soon all the other children are
safely in too, while the storm rages outside.

By the time Coire arrives at the Base Station, the Press are there. Photographers click and flash their cameras, TV film crews follow Coire and Cairn all afternoon, journalists interview Stroma the Driver and lots of passengers.

'Don't know what we'd have done without the train,' says the expedition leader, as an ambulance takes the boy to hospital.

Next day Coire and Cairn are on the front pages of every newspaper and all over the TV too.

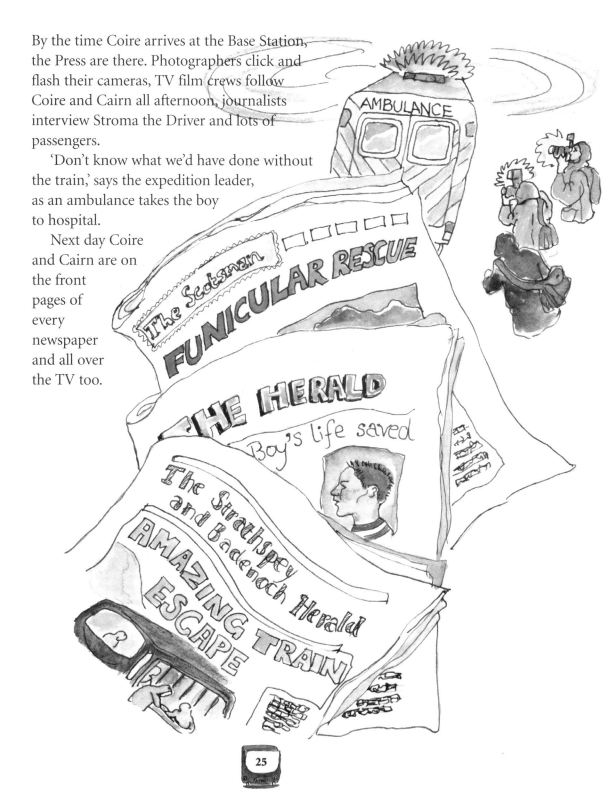

The Scotsman
FUNICULAR RESCUE

THE HERALD
Boy's life saved

The Strathspey and Badenoch Herald
AMAZING TRAIN ESCAPE

In November it's time for Coire and Cairn to take a few days off. Eric the Engineer and his team do maintenance work on the engines, the wheels, the tracks and the brakes.

The weather is colder now and soon the snow begins to fall.

'It's our birthday,' sings Coire on 23rd December. 'We've been here a whole year.'

Next day, Cairn says, 'It's Christmas Eve. Magic things happen on Christmas Eve. I wonder what we'll do?'

Christmas Eve
is indeed special, for that is the night when, just
for a few brief hours, everything comes alive
and all the machines, the toys and even the
animals, can talk to each other and play.

Coire and Cairn
seize their chance to
have some fun.
'Look at me,' sings Coire, 'I'm
snowboarding!'
    Cairn yells, 'And I'm a downhill racer. Watch out!'

But, by the time dawn is breaking on Christmas Day, Coire and Cairn are resting quietly beside each other at the passing place.

'I'm so happy here,' yawns Coire.

Cairn says, 'Me too.'

Stroma the Driver comes on duty. 'We've had a great year. Thanks to both of you. Happy Christmas.'